THIS CANDLEWICK BOOK BELONGS TO:

_____

_____

_____

_____

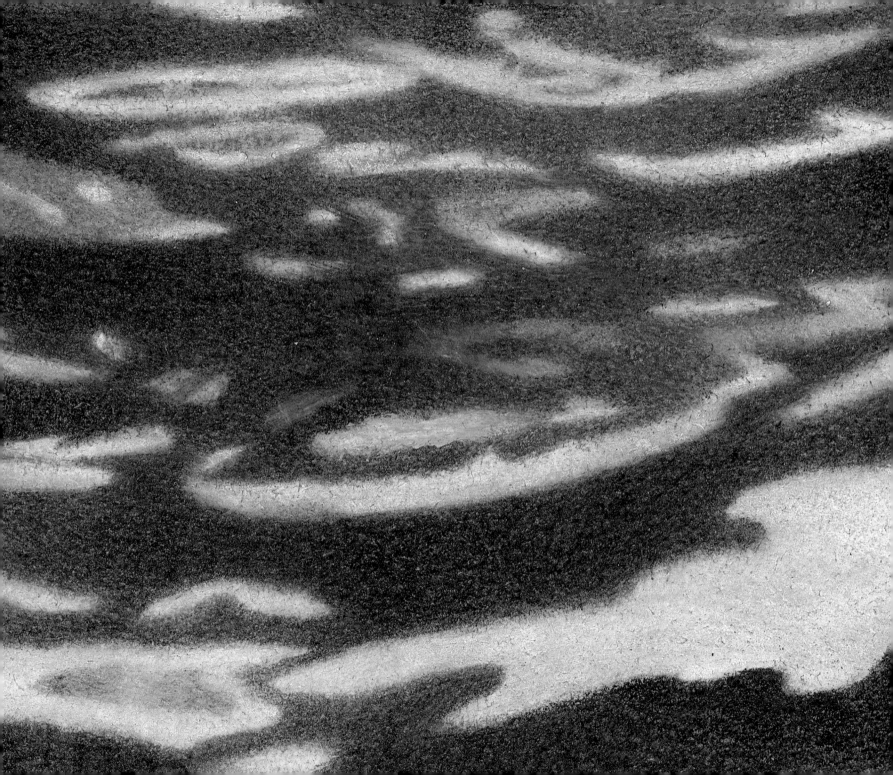

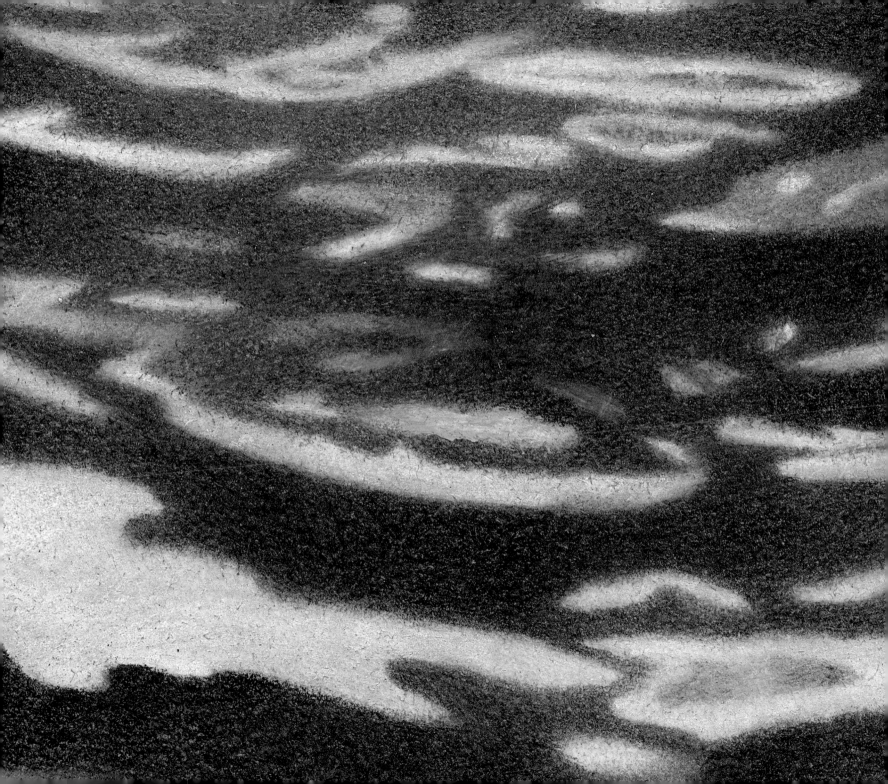

*For D. L.*
**M. W.**

*For Helen Elizabeth*
**J. E.**

Text copyright © 1994 by Martin Waddell
Illustrations copyright © 1994 by Jennifer Eachus

First U.S. paperback edition 1998

The Library of Congress has cataloged the hardcover edition as follows:

Waddell, Martin.
The big big sea / Martin Waddell ; illustrated by Jennifer Eachus.—1st U.S. ed.
p.  cm.
Summary: A young girl and her mother take a nighttime walk to the sea,
creating beautiful memories of a special experience.
ISBN 1-56402-066-5 (hardcover)
[1. Seashore—Fiction.  2. Mothers and daughters—Fiction.  3. Walking—Fiction.]
I. Eachus, Jennifer, ill.  II. Title.
PZ7.W1137Bi    1994
[E]—dc20    93-33228

ISBN 0-7636-0282-5 (paperback)

2 4 6 8 10 9 7 5 3 1

Printed in Hong Kong

This book was typeset in Bauer Bodoni.
The pictures were done in colored pencil.

Candlewick Press
2067 Massachusetts Avenue
Cambridge, Massachusetts 02140

# The Big Big Sea

by
## MARTIN WADDELL

illustrated by
## JENNIFER EACHUS

CANDLEWICK PRESS
CAMBRIDGE MASSACHUSETTS

Mama said, "Let's go!"
So we went . . .

out of the house
and into the dark
and I saw . . .
THE MOON.

We went over the field
and under the fence
and I saw
the sea in the moonlight,
waiting for me.

And I ran
and Mama ran.
We ran and we ran,
straight through the puddles
and out to the sea!

I went right in
to the shiny bit.
There was only me
in the big big sea.

I splashed
and I laughed
and Mama came after me
and we paddled
out deep in the water.

We got all wet.

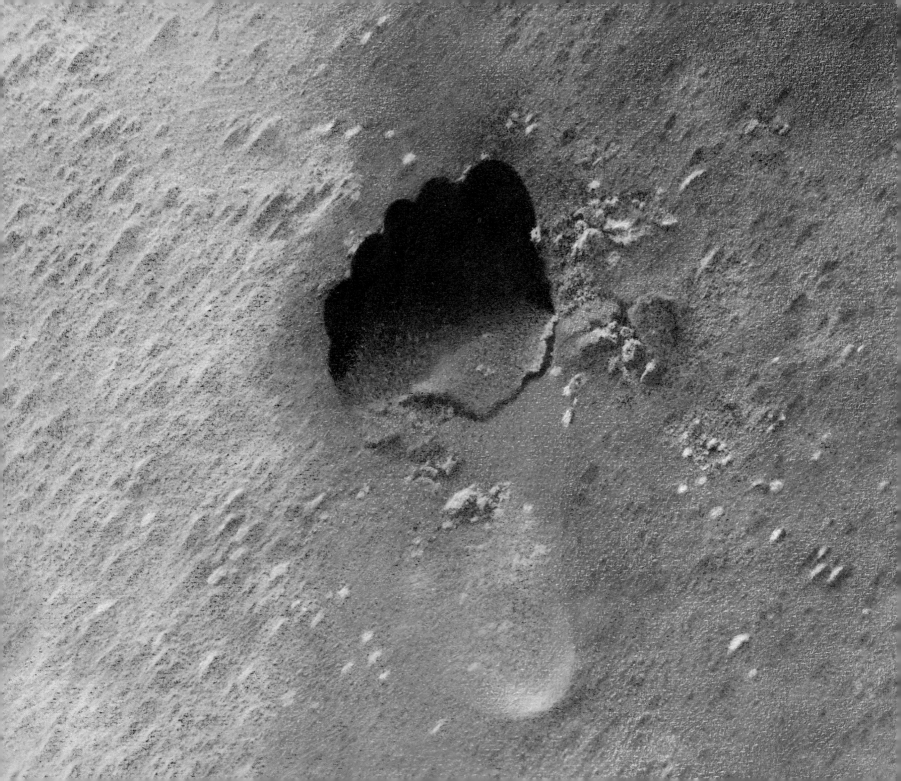

Then we walked
a bit more
by the edge of the sea
and our feet
made big holes
in the sand.

Far far away,
right around the bay,
were the town
and the lights
and the mountains.
We felt very small,
Mama and me.

We didn't go to the town.
We just stayed for a while
by the sea.

And Mama said to me,
"Remember this time.
It's the way life should be."

I got cold
and Mama carried me
all the way back.

We sat by the fire,
Mama and me,
and ate hot buttered toast
and I went to sleep
on her knee.

I'll always remember
just Mama and me
and the night
that we walked
by the big big sea.

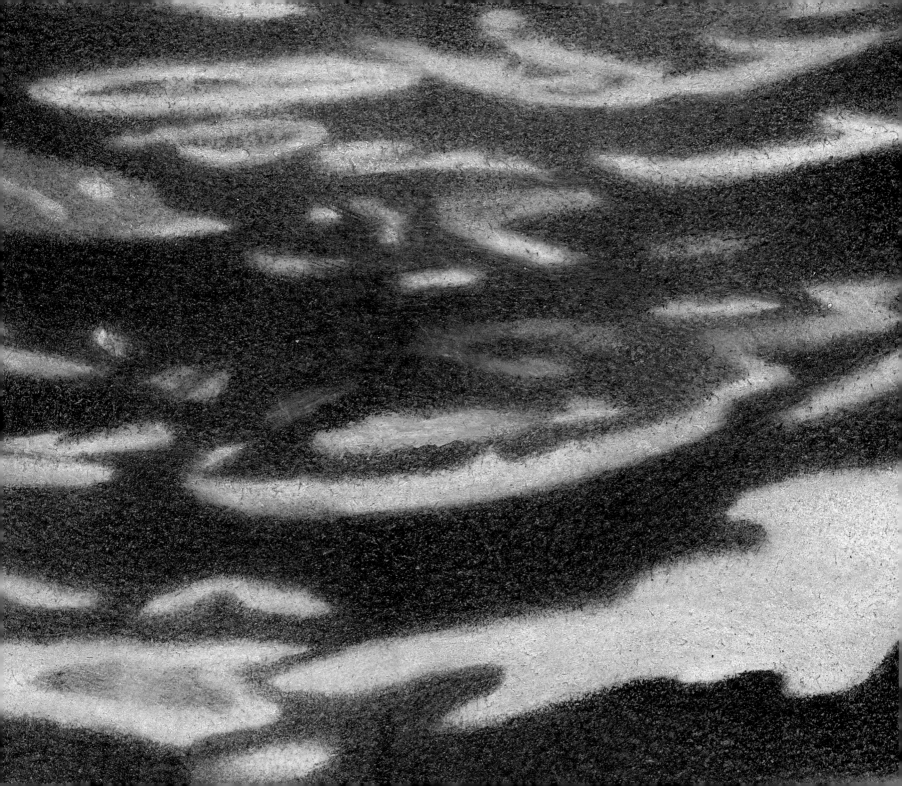

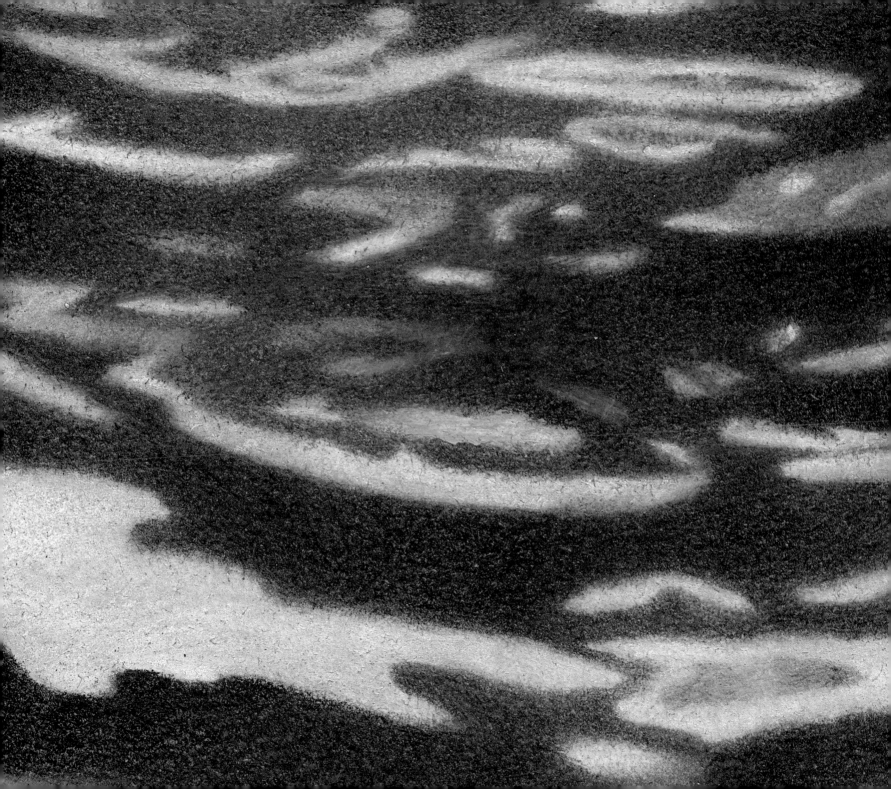

MARTIN WADDELL has written more than one hundred books for children, including *Can't You Sleep, Little Bear?*; *Farmer Duck*; and *Owl Babies*. He was inspired to write *The Big Big Sea* while planning a visit for a friend and her young daughter. He thought that a nighttime walk on the beach would be a perfect experience for both mother and child. After all, he notes, "the moments we share are the moments that stay with us." The book is set "where the mountains of Mourne sweep down to the sea," near Martin Waddell's home in Northern Ireland.

JENNIFER EACHUS was a teacher before becoming an illustrator. Illustrating *The Big Big Sea*, she says, was challenging until she traveled to Northern Ireland to see the beach where the author lives. "I went," she recalls, "when I knew there was to be a full moon. And when I walked out onto the beach, it was exactly as he wrote it. I knew what he was writing about then." Jennifer Eachus is also the illustrator of *In the Middle of the Night*.